D0835753

A catalogue record for this book is available from the British Library

Published by Ladybird Books Ltd
27 Wrights Lane London W8 5TZ
A Penguin Company
2 4 6 8 10 9 7 5 3 1

LADYBIRD and the device of a Ladybird are trademarks of Ladybird Books Ltd

TM & © 2000 DreamWorks L.L.C.,
Aardman Chicken Run Limited and Pathè Image.

Printed in Italy

CHICKEN RUN ™

Book of the Film

As night fell over Tweedy's Farm, a chicken named Ginger – tired of being cooped up like a prisoner – was making her latest daring escape attempt. She dashed across the barnyard to the barbed wire fence, whipped out a spoon, and started digging. When the hole was big enough, she crawled under the fence. Then, at her signal, five other hens rushed out from the shadows. Bunty, the biggest bird of them all, climbed into the hole – and found she couldn't move! "BRAAAAAK!" she squawked. "I'm stuck!"

The hens pushed and pulled at Bunty, but it was no good. Mr Tweedy caught Ginger outside the fence, scooped her up and dumped her into the coal bin for a night of solitary confinement.

Ginger was released just in time for morning roll call.
Mr Tweedy booted her into the chicken yard.

"Morning, Ginger," said silly Babs. "Back from holiday?"

"I wasn't on holiday, Babs!" Ginger retorted. "I was in
solitary confinement!"

"It's nice to get a bit of time for yourself, isn't it?"
said Babs.

Fowler, the farm's rooster, called the
chickens to attention so Mr and Mrs
Tweedy could begin the
daily egg count.

But one hen, Edwina, hadn't laid any for three days in a row. The other hens looked on helplessly as Edwina was taken away by Mr Tweedy. At Tweedy's, if you weren't a layer, you were dinner!

Now Ginger was more determined than ever to escape. That night, she called a secret meeting to discuss new plans.

At the escape committee meeting, Ginger and Mac
– chief engineer and Ginger's right-hand hen –
demonstrated their latest plan with the help of a
turnip. They would build a catapult and go over the
fence. The room filled with nervous clucking as the
turnip smashed against the wall. This was the
craziest plan yet!

"Face the facts, ducks," said Bunty. "The chances
of us getting out of here are a million to one!"

"Then there's still a chance!" Ginger said. But
deep down she feared she would never be able to
lead her fine feathered friends to freedom.

Discouraged, Ginger left the hut. "Heaven, help us," she sighed.

Suddenly, she heard a cry of "Freedom!" She looked up to see a rooster flying through the air before crash-landing in the barnyard. A piece of a poster advertising "Rocky the Flying Rooster" floated down after him – and Ginger's heart soared. She'd hatched a new plan.

The hens rushed Rocky inside and bandaged his sprained wing as Ginger explained her idea – Rocky would teach them to fly! But Rocky's plans didn't include sticking around a chicken farm. "The open road – that's more my style," he said. "Just give me

a pack on my back, and point me where the wind blows."

Rocky was about to escape when a circus van pulled up. He was on the run from the circus! Thinking quickly, Ginger made a deal: the hens would hide Rocky, if he taught them how to fly. Rocky had no choice but to help them out.

The next morning, Rocky began training the flock. The hens all worked hard to get in shape, but after a few days still no one could lift a feather off the ground.

"Relax, we're making progress," said Rocky. But as Nick and Fetcher, the farmyard rats, kept laughing at the hens' failed attempts, Ginger started to have a sinking feeling about Rocky.

Meanwhile, strange things were happening on the farm. A truck delivered a huge crate, and Mrs Tweedy started measuring the chickens instead of counting eggs. Then the food rations were doubled, sending the hens into an eating frenzy. Finally, Ginger got the picture. Mrs Tweedy was fattening them up! She was going to kill them all. But how?

Rocky came up with a plan of his own. He decided that the chickens needed a little fun to cheer them up. By promising Nick and Fetcher the next egg he laid, Rocky conned the two sneaky rats into stealing a radio – the rats didn't realise that roosters don't lay eggs!

Soon the hens were dancing to the music. Even Ginger took a turn with Rocky on the dance floor. With all the flapping and twirling, Babs suddenly became airborne! Her flight only lasted a moment, but it renewed the chickens' hope.

"Looks like I owe you an apology," said Ginger. "I didn't think you cared about us, but after all this, it seems I was wrong."

Rocky was about to tell Ginger the truth about his flying skills, when suddenly a deafening rumble was heard from the barn.

Mr and Mrs Tweedy had turned on their new money-making pie machine. Soon, every store in the county would be stocked with Mrs Tweedy's Homemade Chicken Pies!

"How does it work?" asked Mr Tweedy.

"Get me a chicken and I'll show you," Mrs Tweedy snarled.

Before she could shake a feather, Ginger was snapped up, strapped onto a conveyer belt, and heading straight into the machine!

Fearlessly, Rocky charged in after her. Dodging rotating saw blades and mixed vegetables, he grabbed Ginger and they made their escape – but not before sabotaging the machine.

Back in the hut, Ginger told the hens about the
terrible pie-making machine. The chickens started
to panic.

"I don't want to be a pie!" shrieked Babs. "I don't
like gravy!"

Ginger calmed them down by promising that
Rocky would show them how to fly the next day.
Soon they would be free!

Later, Ginger thanked Rocky for saving her life.
Rocky tried once again to tell her his secret, but he
just couldn't get the words out.

ROCKY
THE
FLYING
CHICKEN SPECTACULAR
IN TOWN
FOR ONE WEEK ONLY
Two Performances
DAILY 4.45 • 7.45 SATURDAY 2.30 • 5.30
GRAND NORTHERN TOUR
BOOK NOW
Seeing is Believing!
COL.
SPOON'S

The hens couldn't wait to see Rocky fly. But when Ginger went to find Rocky the next morning, all she found was the bottom half of his poster. It showed him being fired out of a circus cannon. Ginger realized the truth. Rocky couldn't fly after all!

She broke the bad news to the hens. "Let's face it," she said. "The only way out of here is wrapped in pastry!"

Discouraged, the hens began to squabble and fight. As Fowler stepped in to break it up, Ginger realized something. Fowler was in the Royal Air Force!

Filled with inspiration, Ginger told them all her latest plan. They'd build an aeroplane – just like the ones Fowler had flown!

With no time to lose, the hens got organized. Everyone lent a hand. In exchange for eggs from Bunty, Nick and Fetcher helped the chickens steal tools from right under Mr Tweedy's nose.

Seeing the hens so energized filled Ginger with pride. But it also made her realize something. She missed Rocky.

Meanwhile, out on his own, Rocky was realizing something too. Freedom could be a lonely road to follow. Spotting a huge billboard advertising Mrs Tweedy's Chicken Pies, Rocky began to question his decision to desert Ginger and the other hens in their time of need.

Back in the barnyard, the chickens froze in fear as the repaired pie machine roared into life again. When Mr Tweedy came to get them, Ginger cried "Attack!" and the hens swooped on him. They trussed him up and wheeled the flying machine out onto a runway lit by a string of Christmas lights. The time had come to make their escape!

But there was a problem: Fowler was a mascot in the RAF, not a pilot. "The Royal Air Force doesn't let chickens behind the controls of a complex aircraft!" he explained.

Ginger convinced him to take the controls, and as the plane approached the take-off ramp, Mr Tweedy struggled up and kicked it over. Then Mrs Tweedy appeared, looming over Ginger with an axe. But before she could swing, a loud noise distracted her.

It was Rocky, riding a tricycle! He sailed over the fence, and knocked Mrs Tweedy to the ground.

Rocky and Ginger quickly put the ramp in place. As the plane took off, Rocky and Ginger grabbed hold of the dangling lights and scrambled aboard. Annoyed at Rocky for leaving, Ginger slapped him. Then, happy to have him back, she leant in to kiss him.

As she did so, the plane jolted. Mrs Tweedy had grabbed hold of the lights too! Ginger leant out to cut the lights free, but before she knew it, she and Mrs Tweedy were dangling behind the plane!

As Ginger tried to cut Mrs Tweedy off, the woman was hit in the face with something – an egg! Rocky was attacking Mrs Tweedy with the help of Nick and Fetcher.

But they didn't have enough eggs! Mrs Tweedy raised the axe, and swung at Ginger. In the nick of time, Ginger ducked, and the axe sliced through the string of lights, sending Mrs Tweedy tumbling down – through the roof of the barn and into the pie machine!

The plane soared up and away from the barn.